JAGUAR

'even the thousand-mile road
has a first step'

Scholastic Children's Books,
Commonwealth House,
1-19 New Oxford Street, London WC1A 1NU
A division of Scholastic Limited
London ~ New York ~ Toronto ~ Sydney ~ Auckland

First published by Scholastic Children's Books in 1997

ISBN 0 590 54258 3

Printed in Hong Kong

10 9 8 7 6 5 4 3 2 1

JAGUAR

HELEN COWCHER

SCHOLASTIC
PRESS

At dusk, a silent figure casts his gaze
forward and back across the lagoon.

That same evening on the plain,
a rider making his way home,
sees marks left in the dust.

In his mind he sees his herd.
He is worried. He's used to losing
cattle from sickness and drought.
But this is different.

His herd is under new threat from
an ancient foe, stalking his land,
but possessed of a mystical power
which holds sway over his thoughts.

Very early next morning, he sets off
along the dry river bed,
stealthily searching
all the while.

As the man walks, Jaguar swims
from his island hide-out.
Suddenly razor-sharp teeth pierce his tail.
Piranhas!
Biting and snapping!
Jaguar swims on, soon
escaping his tormentors.

Anaconda stirs . . .
Jaguar swims on, unaware of
this deadly enemy beneath him!

On another shore, a basking caiman bares
his teeth, completely still.
As the day becomes hotter,
the man hunts in earnest,
soaking in signs with all his senses.

Quietly and carefully,
he follows Jaguar into the forest.

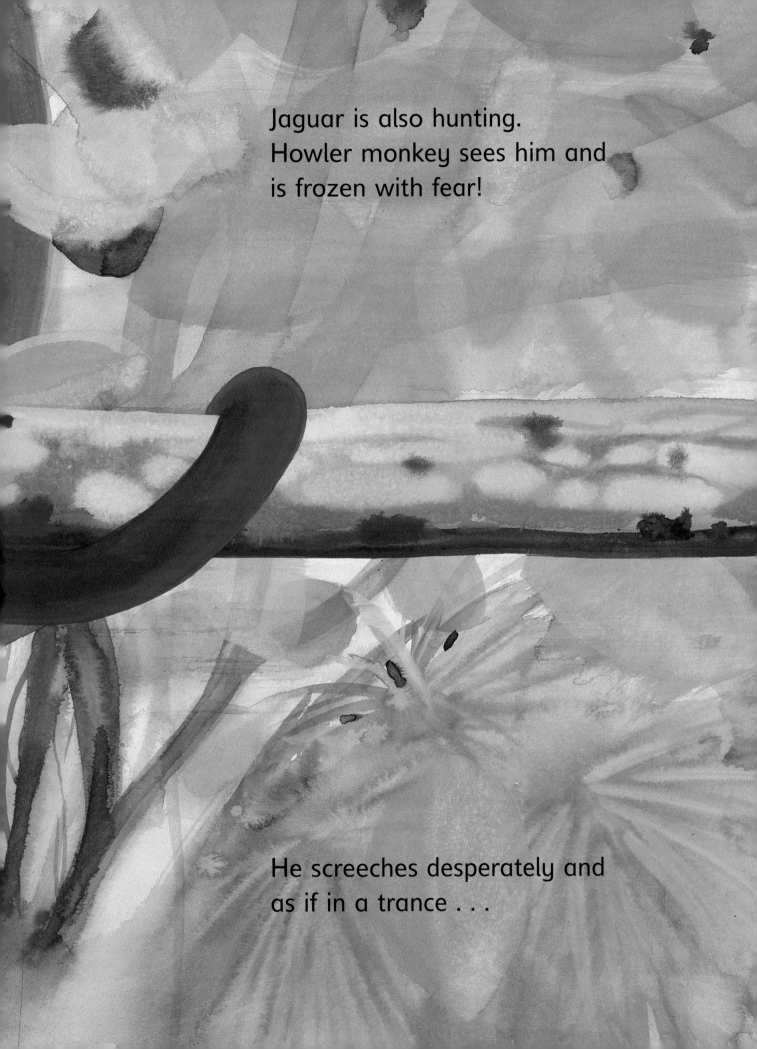

Jaguar is also hunting.
Howler monkey sees him and
is frozen with fear!

He screeches desperately and
as if in a trance . . .

. . . loses his grip
and tumbles to the ground.
Jaguar's search for food
is over for a while.

The day is hot, the pool is cool.
Noisy hoatzin and chachalacas
cease their chatter. Jaguar bathes.

As Jaguar relaxes his guard,
an eye is trained upon him.
The man's quest is over,
yet he feels uneasy.
It is rare for him to see
such a beautiful animal.

The hunter holds his gun firm,
but his mind is troubled.
He fixes his sight and prepares
to fire but he cannot shoot.

Once, he recalls, our forests
and vast plains used to hide many
big cats and now there are few.
Against our dogs and guns they
stood no chance.
Their natural power counted for nothing!

It is as if the glade has cast
its spell upon him.

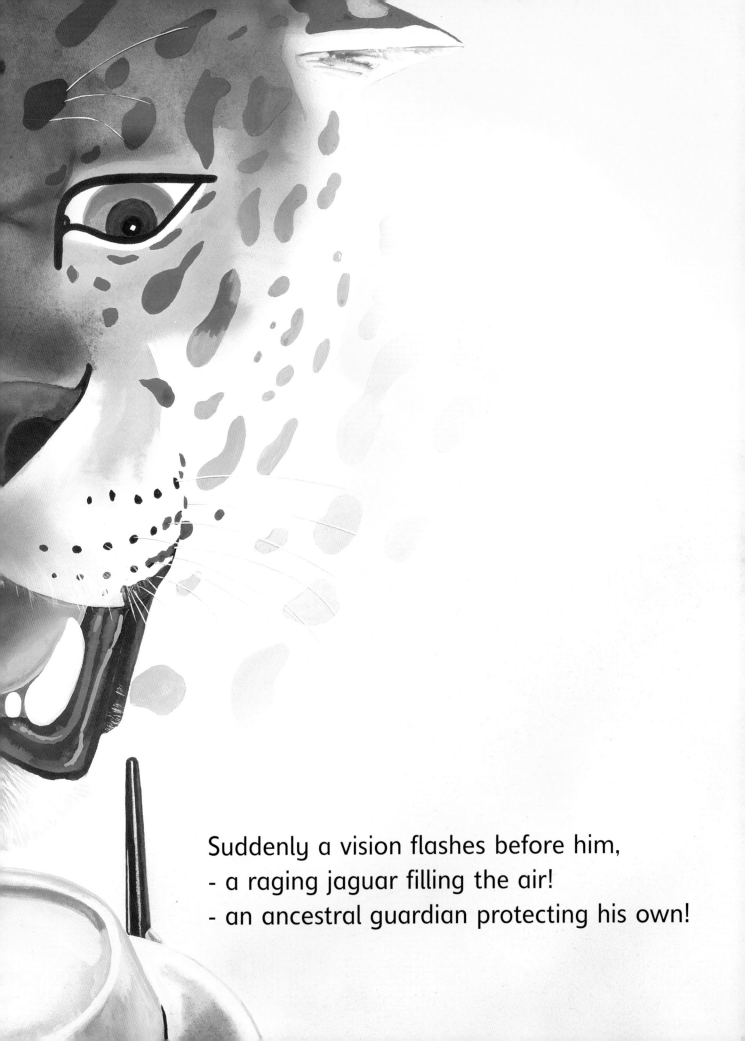

Suddenly a vision flashes before him,
- a raging jaguar filling the air!
- an ancestral guardian protecting his own!

The hunter's will to kill deserts him.
He sinks to his knees in wonder at
such power and beauty.

He does not even hear the sound of
lapping water as, behind the trees
and undisturbed, the jaguar he had
come to kill leaves the pool.

Scarlet macaws fly over the man as
he makes his way back through the forest.
He feels no regret.
His mind is full of his vision
and his heart has softened.

He has discovered a different sort
of courage. He will find other ways
to keep his herds safe.
The land belongs to the jaguar
as much as to him.

More About Jaguar

WHY WAS HOWLER MONKEY SO FRIGHTENED?

- All animals fear the jaguar, but howler monkeys have an especially deep fear.

- Sometimes a howler monkey becomes a willing victim. It seems to give up all thought of escape and as if impelled by an invisible force, cries out with alarm and is drawn towards the jaguar!

WHAT ABOUT PIRANHAS, CAIMANS AND ANACONDAS?

- Piranhas are aggressive fish. They always attack in groups, sometimes hundreds at a time. Some jaguars have lost as much as 15cm of their tail to piranhas!

- Spectacled caimans are related more to alligators than crocodiles. They do not attack humans and their main predators are anacondas and jaguars.

- Anacondas always live near water where they like to submerge themselves. An anaconda will lash out, coiling around unsuspecting prey until the victim suffocates.

- This snake digests slowly and after one good-sized meal can survive many months without food.

- It is the largest snake in the world (not the longest, but the most bulky), measuring 5-6 metres and weighing 150kg.

- A fully grown anaconda is dangerous to man and even to a jaguar!

WHY IS JAGUAR SO POWERFUL?

- From Central America as far south as Argentina, Jaguar is at the top of the food chain. This means he has no natural predator apart from man.

- He is the third largest of the world's big cats, reaching 50-100kg in weight.

- His jaw is the most powerful, relative to size, of all the big cats. He can bite straight through the armour-plated shell of a large turtle.

WHAT DOES 'THE RAGING SPIRIT JAGUAR' MEAN TO THE HUNTER?

- Throughout the tropical forests and plains of Central and South America, there is a fear of the jaguar, bordering on worship.

- Although the jaguar is rarely seen, its tracks are often visible, and its roar sounds at night, giving a feeling of menacing presence.

- The jaguar is respected for its physical powers, but belief in its supernatural power is very important too.

- The hunter, in this book, has known a sorcerer who transformed himself into a jaguar.

- He has also heard of the forest indians' initiation rites, during which a boy passes into manhood and sees his 'Spirit Master'. What he sees is important knowledge and must be kept secret.
- For some, the 'Spirit Master' is an eagle, for some a snake, for others a jaguar.
- When a boy knows his 'Spirit Master' is a jaguar, he knows too that his soul has 'jaguar' qualities. He is quick-witted, cunning and strong. And afterwards in the forest, he watches out for the jaguar; for to harm him would be to endanger his own soul.
- The hunter will have heard many stories of such power. He may only half believe them, but nonetheless they affect him.

So when the 'raging jaguar spirit' confronts him, he is both awestruck and afraid.

WHY WOULD A JAGUAR KILL CATTLE?

- A jaguar may roam into new territory where favourite prey, peccary and deer, have been over-hunted by man.
- If there is a road nearby, this is likely. So the jaguar is forced to risk endangering itself by coming closer to man, and taking livestock.
- If a jaguar is old or if it has been wounded in the past, (gun-shot damage to the jaw, for example), then it will not be fit enough to hunt wild prey.

WHY IS THE JAGUAR AN ENDANGERED SPECIES?

- Up until 1970, when the jaguar was officially listed as an endangered species, many thousands were killed for their fur. During the last 3 years before the ban, 30,000 skins were imported into the USA alone!
- Since such trade was made illegal, the threat now comes from the jaguar's shrinking habitat.

WHAT DOES THE FUTURE HOLD?

- The pressure on wilderness from increasing human population is a big problem, especially for the jaguar. Because each jaguar needs a territory of 65 square km in which to roam, there must be very large wild areas left, where jaguars can live and breed.
- One idea is to have large nature reserves connected by smaller areas of wilderness, within which wild creatures can take cover whilst passing from one reserve to another. These are known as 'wilderness corridors'.
- Another idea is to relocate the few jaguars that become accustomed to preying on cattle.
- In Venezuela, a few enlightened cattle ranchers use the combination of wildlife corridors, undisturbed forest and managed pastureland so that cattle, wildlife and eco-tourism can co-exist.

HOW TO FIND OUT MORE:

LIVING EARTH
Warwick House
106 Harrow Road
London W2 1XD
England

WILDLIFE CONSERVATION SOCIETY
2300 Southern Boulevard
Bronx
New York 10460
USA

RAINFOREST ACTION NETWORK
450 Sansome
Suite 700
San Francisco
California 94111
USA

W.W.F (U.K.)
Panda House
Weyside Park
Godalming
Surrey
GU7 1XR
England

1. IGUANA
2. GREAT EGRET
3. SCARLET IBIS
4. CRESTED CARACARA
5. BOAT-BILLED HERON
6. RUFOUS-VENTED CHACHALACA
7. SIDENECK TURTLE
8. YELLOW-KNOBBED CURRASOW
9. CRAB-EATING FOX
10. HOATZIN
11. BLUE MORPHO BUTTERFLY
12. CAPYBARA
13. JABIRU STORK
14 WHITE-TAILED DEER

The Story of *Jaguar*

- *Jaguar* is set in the Venezuelan Llanos, which lies north of the great River Orinoco. In the rainy season, much of it becomes floodplain. In *Jaguar*, it is the dry season.

- In the Llanos, live the Llaneros (cowboys), very skilled horsemen who are used to working in extreme conditions. They work throughout floods, fires, and drought, riding for many hours each day under the intense tropical sun. Often as they ride, they sing songs of their lives on the plains . . . of horses and cattle, of women and romance, and of the beauty of nature, which they see all around them.

GARY HODGES

Helen with Gertrudis "a Llanero who can see a tiny humming bird, even when it's behind him!"

- Their ancestors were either indigenous Indians or Africans or Spaniards. Now their descendants, a mixture of all three races, are justly proud to be Llaneros.

- In 1992, Helen Cowcher joined a group of British and Venezuelan artists to paint the richly diverse habitats of Venezuela. The resulting group exhibition in Caracas raised funds for environmental education.

- Helen Cowcher stayed at HATO PIÑERO in the northern Llanos. This cattle ranch is world famous for its flora and fauna and prides itself in being a model of sustainable development. Helen has returned many times drawn back by the land, the people and the wildlife.

THANK YOU to:
Señor Antonio Julio Branger,
FUNDACIÓN BRANGER
and all at the Biological Station,
Hato Piñero, Ana Jesus,
José Gertrudis Gamarra
and all the other friends in Venezuela,
who have helped me:
LIVING EARTH, TIERRA VIVA
and the BRITISH COUNCIL.

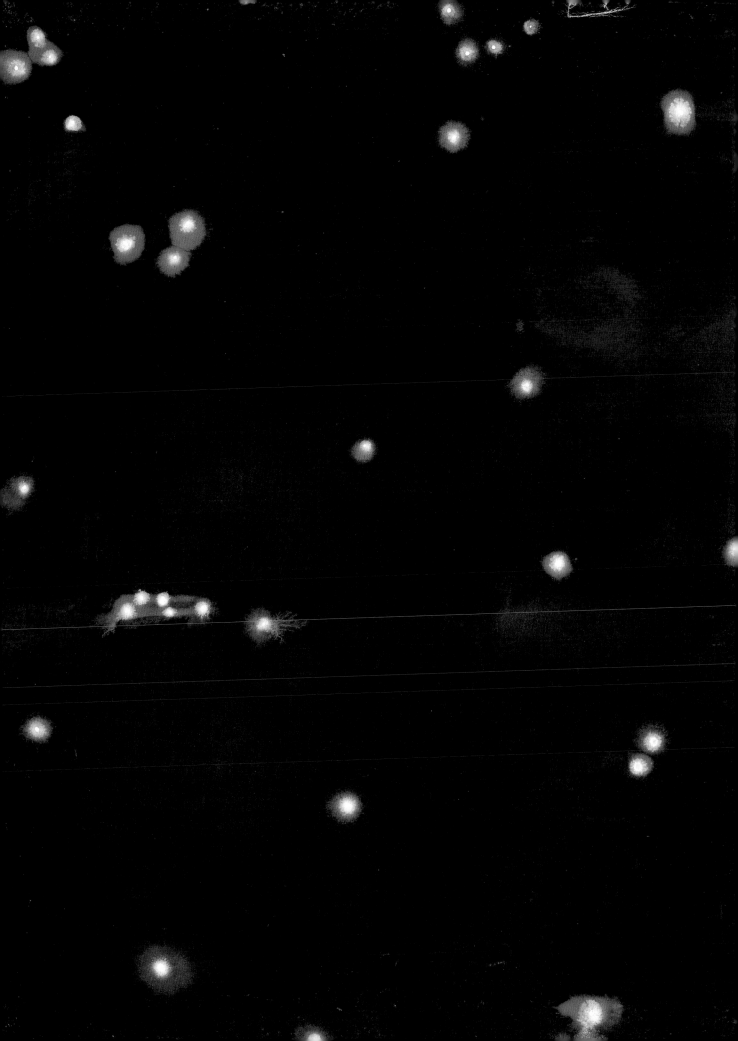